The Dungeon Master's Guide To

AVALON

Part One: Escape from Spindlebark

DUNGEONS OF AVALON

DAN THORNE

AVALON

Contents

AVALON USER MANUAL PART ONE: GAME BASICS

Avalon (TM) is the first multiplayer fantasy Total Immersion (TM) game from Avalon Productions (TM). As such, we recommend you familiarise yourself with the game controls and read this manual carefully before venturing into the starter area of Avalon. As we are sure you are aware, the experience of the game is quite unlike anything else available, and the technology that drives the experience is the most advanced in the market.

Once you enter the game, it will soon become apparent that the immersion process is complete. *You will believe that you are there.* The neural headset hardware (TM) that comes with the game simulation is, of course, tested in all aspects of its performance. You will feel the breeze brushing against your skin, squint at the brightness of the sun if you look at it for too long, and listen to the birds singing in the hedgerows. The experience *is* total, and as such, it is important to remember a few basic commands to begin with.

Some people take longer to adjust to the simulation than others, and although every effort has been made to minimise motion sickness, it is best to limit your play time to short periods at first until you feel that you have adjusted. Having said that, it is generally advisable to never initially play the game for over three hours at a time. We recommend you take frequent breaks.

The command to log out of the game and put the neural headset into standby mode is easy to remember. When in-game, say, "LOG OUT AVALON," and you will be logged out. Be aware that this command will not work if you are in combat, but once combat is ended – whether you win or lose – the command will work once again. Once inside the game, your player "Avatar" will not need food, drink, or sleep, though players can sleep in the game or eat any edible items that they come across. Some even have useful bonuses such as increasing the player's in-game strength, for example! This is just one example of many – and beware! Some items you find, if eaten in-game, can also have a detrimental effect! We do, however, recommend the Urlish beef stew, as it is especially good! Of course, your real-life level of tiredness or mental awareness is reflected in the game. Should you fall asleep while playing the game, you will automatically be logged out and deactivate the neural headset after ten minutes of inaction.

If you die in the game - by losing a fight to a stronger creature than yourself or falling off a cliff, for example - then the game will automatically revive you at a safe distance from whatever killed you. Obviously, the game cannot actually hurt you, and all weapons and strikes by any creatures against your character in the game are not real. You do have a set amount of life points that, when they reach zero, mean that you will die in the game.

Avalon is also unique in that there is no in-game interface. No icons, no health bars, etc, like most games of this type. There is no real interface for a reason (Please see Avalon User Manual: The Game Interface.), but in short, the design team felt that without such an interface, the game would be much more "immediate" – much more "real". In effect, if you find a sword in the game, try swinging it. Combat is a big part of the game, and you will learn to use whatever weapon you choose to use by – well, using it! The more practice that you have in swinging the sword, then the more proficient you will become in using it. This principle is the same as many objects you will find in your adventures!

As you travel through Avalon, you will gain experience points for exploration, completing missions and winning fights against creatures. When your experience level hits maximum, you advance in levels. Higher-level creatures that would kill you outright at lower levels would then slowly become much easier to fight. As you look at enemy creatures you will encounter, you will notice that a creature below your current level has a green haze around it that is just visible when you look at it. If the enemy is the same level as you, then the colour of the haze is blue. If it has a yellow haze surrounding it, it is a slightly higher level than you. Orange is a few levels higher than you and will present a real challenge in overcoming it. Purple-indicated creatures, however, mean that the creature is way out of your league, so beware! If it is grey, however, you will kill it easily, and as such, you will receive no gain in experience from killing it at all.

Weapons can be found on your travels, as can many other items of armour and clothing, as well as many mysterious objects and items. The uses of some of these may not always be immediately apparent, so if in doubt – experiment! Also bear in mind that some items are designed to be used once only, whilst others may have a set purpose – a key for a locked door, for example, will almost certainly only be relevant to use when opening one door only.

Your character will resemble that of the avatar you created on the character creation scheme, or if you so choose, as your real-life self. This is how other players in the game will see you, so choose your colour schemes carefully!

Please Note that unlike many other old-school (That is, non-immersion) games on the market, Avalon has no character classes, and the fighting prowess, magic, etc., is in the game for everyone to discover. For example, you may, over time, become proficient using a sword and shield, but you may at the same time also learn several types of magic spells to aid you in combat.

Experimentation is the key, and there are many secrets to be found in the game!

Please enjoy your time in Avalon, but remember to immerse yourself slowly and take frequent breaks. The neural headset is self-maintaining, but please use common sense when playing Avalon—it is a total immersion experience, and it will take some time to become accustomed to the environment.

Avalon Productions (TM) has spent decades developing the Total Immersion TM system and creating the myths, legends, landscapes and lore of Avalon. We look forward to hearing your feedback, but one thing we know is that you are going to have fun out there!

Happy adventuring!

PART ONE

There never seemed to be enough logs. Pip picked up his axe and, swinging it over his head, buried it deep in the thick tree trunk on the ground in front of him, splitting it in two easily. He wiped his brow and straightened up, giving a slight groan as he did so.

"Seems no end to cutting these up," he muttered to nobody in particular, for he was alone, as indeed he always was. Pausing only to catch his breath, he then cut a few more before carrying them to a huge pile of chopped wood that was stacked up against a small cabin that was itself also made of wood. Beside the cabin was a small well, the bucket of which was currently winched up. On the ground, for no apparent reason at all, were a pair of keys and what looked to be an old-fashioned oil lamp.

Pip sat down on a tree stump beside the path that ran up to the cabin and breathed in deeply, taking in the warm country air. Along the path that led off to the south was a long green hedge, and looking in that direction, it revealed that the cabin sat at the top of a small hill. If you cared to take a good look around, you would also notice that the hill was almost dead centre in a wide green valley, with tall steep hills rising all around. To the north, far in the distance and contrasting starkly against the azure blue and cloudless sky, stood a tall mountain, far, far away, the peak of it topped by clean white snow which was just visible, standing out against the azure sky.

At the eastern end of the valley, a thick forest edged onto the fields, its thick trees seeming to be almost impenetrable. Pip looked around and saw the sheep on the hills high above, and a shepherd attending to them. He started counting logs on the log pile from where he sat, tallying them up so he had an approximate number in his head. When he got to sixty, he stopped counting. That was enough, he knew, because there were a few visitors on the way, he knew instinctively, but not many, and they rarely stayed for long. Once they had the map, they seemed to bugger off, he thought, and good riddance to them! If he had to listen to the complaints of dizziness and shock one more time, he would likely start using the axe to do more than just cut wood.

He sighed deeply and tried to raise his spirits. He knew, of course, that he had no part to play with the axe other than to cut the wood to allow the fires to be lit to complete the first-day party, and beyond that, his duties really were just to show people around. Once they had a peek down that well, they were usually off pretty sharpish, and he was left behind. He sighed once again, stood up, and returned to cutting wood. He knew he had enough and no more to do, but there were two inbound, he felt, so he had to set the scene.

As if on cue, two bright flashes of light appeared, and two people appeared in the clearing, standing less than ten feet away, watching him pretend to cut wood.

"Oh, my God!" the woman half whispered.

Here we go again. Sighed Pip to himself. The woman touched her face, then her arms, then her face again. She took one step forward and staggered slightly, then corrected herself and stood still, taking a deep breath. The man next to her was not in quite as much disarray. In fact, he was laughing and looking around in amazement.

"I can feel the breeze moving through my hair," she whispered rather over-loudly, Pip thought. "Oh my God. I can smell the flowers and…" she turned around, swaying as she did so. "... and the…. Yuk! Is that smell coming from the fields?" She looked startled a little, seeing the man nearly beside her for the first time, but quickly recovered.

"Not playing the game together, then." Thought Pip.

"They must be readying the field for crops." said the man, stepping forward and raising his hand up to the sun so he could look out across the valley without having to blink furiously.

"It's December," she said.

"Not here." smiled the man. "It's never any particular season here, really."

"You have been here before?" asked the woman, still swaying.

"Not as such," said the man with a smile, "but I read the manual." He looked around, wide-eyed, taking in all of his surroundings. "And the reviews as well, of course."

"Ah," she said, raising her head up to the sky and instantly regretting doing so. "If you read the manual, that makes you a geek in my book. I thought men didn't read manuals?"

"It's always a good idea if you are entrusting every one of your senses to a simulation," smiled the man, holding out his hand to her.

"Tom."

"Morgus." said the woman, shaking his hand and blushing slightly.

"Is that your in-game name?" he asked, and she nodded. "Ah. Okay. Tom is my real name."

"Anyone ever call you Tommy?"

"Not if they want me to answer them." he smiled. She grinned, noticing him smiling back at her for the first time. He was of average height, she thought, maybe five-ten, quite slim and had short black hair. Brown eyes. Not her type, really, but it probably wasn't what he looked like in real life anyway. She smiled briefly, coming to terms with the fact that she was just looking at an avatar he had created for himself. He might not even be a "he"! She could not resist asking.

"So you are a man, yes?"

"What?"

"A man. In real life. You *are* a man, aren't you?"

"Of course I am a man."

"Well, it pays to ask," she laughed. " For all I know, you could be a twenty-stone female wrestler. I could be a lorry driver."

Tom looked at her long blonde hair and figure and considered that it was impossible to tell. He was just looking at a construct made by the person playing the game. During the lengthy character creation process that the game demanded before you could even enter the game world, he had considered creating a female character but had changed his mind at the last moment. He had reasoned that the game's major selling point was how real the experience was, and so to not play the game as his real gender seemed almost a cop-out.

He saw that they were both dressed in what looked like standard in-game clothing, both roughly the same and comprising of leather trousers and boots, a leather jerkin and a wide belt tied about their respective waists. The belt had an empty scabbard at one end and a small pouch at the other.

"I am not a twenty-stone female wrestler!" he laughed. "This is really me. I couldn't be bothered with all the character creation options. I let the game auto-generate my appearance based on what I actually really look like. I just wanted to see if this was as real as every review I have read said it was. It seemed unlikely." He looked around, sniffing the scent of pine rising from the forest below, borne on the breeze and across the valley.

"I have the feeling that we haven't seen anything yet." he smiled and took a few steps forward.

"You definitely do sound as if you have been here before."

"Not at all," he protested. "I am a sucker for the promotional material - not to mention the television advertisements. Apart from that, I have read everything on the system as well. Seen all the system demos since the first press release. Having said all of that, in truth, I am just as gobsmacked as you."

She reached down and ran her fingers through the grass.

"Oh, my," she said, straightening up again and this time not swaying at all. "It feels real."

"Well, when you look at the tech years they spent getting everything right, the investment is incredible. They do say that the company needs an Avalon neural headset in every home just to break even."

"Do they?"

"Yes. Are you surprised? Look at the sheep up in the hills. The snow on the mountain on the horizon." He looked up. The birds overhead." He saw her nodding in awe. Then, they both saw Pip standing by the well and the cabin to one side. "The woodcutter," he finished, and Pip smiled and strode across to shake their hands.

It was an interesting task for Pip, who was no more than four feet in height and, although quite stocky, presumably because of the constant wood cutting, could hardly be described as an imposing character.

"Are you a hobbit?" said Morgus, a look of awe on her face. Pip smiled patiently.

"The Avalon company would like to make it known that any resemblance to hobbits, stated or inferred, is merely a coincidence and that all of the copyright regulations regarding hobbits are copyright of the Tolkien Estate and in no way whatsoever represented in any part of the Avalon environment in any shape or form," he said in an obviously previously written and carefully scripted statement, his voice fast and monotone in equal measures. The woman's eyes slowly crossed as he spoke but shot back into focus as he concluded his spiel.

"Not a hobbit then," said Tom, and Pip shook his head.

"Welcome to Spindlebark!" he said, sweeping his arms around the vista, smiling broadly. "This is the southernmost province of Southmere in the land of Avalon. I am Pip, a humble woodcutter and guide who will assist you in your orientation and first steps in Avalon. May they be many and fruitful."

"It's nice to meet you," said Tom, holding out a hand that the small man shook enthusiastically. Morgus held her hand out as well, and her eyes went wide as the man shook.

"Feels so real," she said to Tom, and he nodded.

"Pleased to meet you too," said Pip. "I was just cutting some wood for the welcome party this evening. Luckily, I finished it all, so I don't need any help with that." They both looked at the pile of wood stacked against the cabin. "Are either of you feeling unwell, experiencing any feelings of motion sickness, or simply overwhelmed by the experience upon arriving here today?"

"I'm good," said Tom. I'm pretty impressed so far." Pip nodded and looked at the woman.

"I think I'm okay," she said. I know how to go offline if it all gets too much."

"Excellent," said Pip, smiling. You have second-guessed me there. Remember: all you have to say is "LOGOUT AVALON," and you will be disconnected, and the neural headset will power down instantly.

"Okay," they both said in unison, and Pip visibly relaxed now that the formalities were out of the way. Come and take a look at the well," said Pip, and they both tentatively followed him, approaching the small brick well. The roof was wood, and the bucket was on the floor, a small winch ready to lower and raise it. "Use the winch and bucket to get some water if you wish."

Pip turned the winch, and as he did so, the bucket vanished down into the well. There was a slight splash from within the stone-lined pit, and then Pip reversed the direction of the winch, and the bucket soon appeared again, full of water.

"Try it," he said. "It's quite cold. Very refreshing."

Tom allowed Morgus to taste it first by cupping some of the

water in his hands and raising it to her mouth. She looked puzzled, and Tom did the same, smiling as he drank the water.

"It doesn't taste of anything. Not synthetic, nothing preserved or added." he said, "Just water. Apparently, the taste of the food is the same." He smiled, wiping his lips. "Or so the brochures say."

"Now that I can't wait to try," she said. "Food that tastes as it should, but no calories at all. Every dieter's dream."

"Yes. Can't wait to try it myself either," said Tom. They looked around and noticed the keys and lantern on the floor. Tom reached for both at exactly the same time that Morgus did. The resulting sensation was, they both thought, very curious. They both now held a lamp and a bunch of keys, but at the same time, the two objects were still on the floor in front of them.

"Universal objects." smiled Tom. "They are available for all players. Some aren't, I believe. That's why we both have one."

"Well, what are the keys for?" she asked, and Tom pointed at the door.

"Ladies first."

"Charmed, I am sure," she said and, placing the first key in the lock, turned it. Nothing happened. The bunch had six keys on it, and the fourth one she tried opened the door. They walked inside the small shed to see a small display of weapons on the wall, ranging from daggers to short swords, long swords that must have been two-handed, as well as several bows and a few small round shields.

"Time to kit up," said Tom, selecting a small shield and sword from the wall. He placed the shield on his back via a short leather strap and placed the sword into the scabbard at his waist. He then selected a small backpack and slung it over his shoulder.

"I don't know what to take." she said, "I wouldn't have a clue about how to use any of these."

"I think you will need a backpack to start with to stow anything you find as you progress." He picked one off the wall and handed it to her. How about a bow? There is a quiver here, too."

"I'm not sure my aim is not up to much," she said, taking the bag off him and placing it on her shoulder.

"I think the more you use it, the more accurate you get, so the choice is not terribly important. I'm no dab hand with a sword and shield; you can be sure of that. In fact, it's the first time I have ever used one. I guess that it's just a preference. The game gets more accurate as you use the weapon more."

"Okay," she said, walking along the rack.

"These are all very basic weapons," said Pip seriously, "there are much more advanced ones available you will find on your travels. I would suggest trying them all out. Spindlebark is a very forgiving village. Not many hazards here at all. Quite a gentle place, in fact. Use it to pick out what suits you best."

Morgus picked the bow, slung a quiver full of arrows over her back, and placed what looked like a short dagger in her belt.

"They aren't heavy or cumbersome," she said, puzzled.

"They aren't real," laughed Tom, and she frowned before smiling.

"Excellent," said Pip, walking back out into the sunshine. As they did so, the door to the cabin slowly swung shut, and there was a quiet click as it locked itself. "Now, maybe take a walk in the hills or across the valley. Don't worry. It won't start to get dark for a few hours yet, and the valley will not likely let you wander too far off the beaten track. I will go and cook a hearty meal to welcome you this evening. Just wander back to this cabin when you are ready." he pointed up the hill to a line of trees where a small hut that they had both previously noticed could just be seen. "My home is there. Return when you are ready."

"Thanks, Pip," said Tom and they both watched as he walked up the hill, singing to himself as he went.

"What happens if I log out right now?" she asked.

"The game just carries on from where you left it when you logged off the next time that you play again," he said. "Pip will still be cooking, and you will still have a little time before he is ready for you. Once logged off, when you return, everything is precisely as you left it in terms of the game itself."

"What about you?" she asked.

"Well, I am real, so I wouldn't be here." he laughed, "That's the only difference. If you logged out now when you returned, it would still be the same time, and Pip would still be preparing the welcome party, but of course, I would not be here unless I logged back in at the same time as you did. Same with any other players, of course, of which there could be thousands."

"Oh. Okay," she said and then frowned. "Of course. Silly me! How did I think it was going to work!" She looked around. "Only seems to be you and I here, though."

"It looks that way," he replied. "Perhaps the game does that at first—keeps you separate from too many other players to avoid swamping you." He looked around the valley, shielding his eyes from the strong, warm sun. "Are you in any particular rush?" he asked, and she shook her head.

"Not at all. It's just that they said in the little bit of the manual that I read it was best to limit your first session to thirty minutes."

"Yes, they do say that," he conceded, "But are you having any problems?" She shook her head. "Motion sickness?" Again, she indicated not.

"Come on, then." Let's climb this hill and see what we can see. If nothing else, we can assess just how accurate a computer-generated sheep is."

"Okay." she smiled, and so they climbed the high hill up the valley, the sheep above growing in size as they slowly climbed the hill.

As they climbed the hill, the world grew around them. The valley floor from where they had ascended was but the smallest part of the landscape. To the north, at the end of the valley in which they stood, they saw rolling fields and pastures as far as the eyes could see. Far beyond that, on the horizon, was the elusive snow-topped mountain, whilst, to the east and northeast, they saw wide forests and rivers heading in those directions. South and west continued as far as the valley did, but beyond that, it was shrouded in a pale grey mist.

"That's the edge of the map," said Tom. Morgus frowned. "If we walked that way, there would be a hill we couldn't climb or a chasm that would stop us."

"Everything lies north then," she said.

"For now, yes. Of course, we have to complete this starting area for now. Learn the basics."

"How do we do that?" she asked.

"Well, let's see," said Tom, pointing to the figure of a man dressed in what looked like a shepherd's smock who was rushing towards them as they spoke.

"Help me, help me!" he cried as he threw himself at their feet, "Old Daisy, Mary, Winita and Flo have only gone and got out of their pens! What with the bad old wolf Ripper about the place they are bound to be eaten before nightfall! Will you help me, master and mistress?"

"Of course," said Tom, winking at Morgus, who was doing her best not to laugh. "Daisy. Mary, Winita and erm… Flo. They are your family, I take it?"

The shepherd laughed as he rose to his feet.

"Oh no, sir," he said, "They are my sheep." he leaned in close and drew them both close in together, "Though they are as good as family. A magnificent animal is a sheep." He tapped his nose conspiratorially. "None too bright, though. Not like a wolf. Cunning wolves are, and that one I call Ripper particularly. Wicked creature, that one. Likes nothing more than to cause a bit of mischief, does old Ripper."

"Ah." said Tom as Morgus wrinkled her nose, "So you want us to round up your sheep and place them back in that pen up the hill?"

"Just so, sir," said the shepherd, "And if you could keep an eye out for that wily old wolf Ripper and sort him out once and for all, then I would be extremely grateful. Thank you, sir and madam, too. Good luck to you both."

The shepherd ran back to his pen as Tom looked about for stray sheep.

"There is one just atop the hill," she said, and so they set off in that direction, though as they approached, they saw that there were many sheep atop the hill, but four of them seemed to be much nearer to them than the others, and every time they moved closer to the flock it seemed to move further away, whereas the four separate sheep did not. Finally, they reached a small white sheep that stood looking at them; its legs braced against the grass as if it was going to take flight at any second.

"Very realistic sheep," said Morgus, "If not a little docile."

"I think that the game is being kind to us," said Tom and he jumped forward and grabbed the sheep, picking it up easily. It hardly struggled at all. "Now, let's find one for you. I think this is going to take two trips." They walked a little further and found another sheep. Morgus grabbed hold of it and easily picked it up. They walked down the hill to the pen, placed the two sheep inside it, and then returned to the top of the hill. They spied two more docile-looking sheep not too far away; however, they also spotted a large black shape stalking through the grass, belly to the ground.

"Ripper," The farmer called him." said Morgus, "The wolf."

"That's a wolf," said Tom. As he looked, he saw a yellow haze flash above its head. "It is yellow, so we should be okay with tackling it. It's just slightly above our level."

"Which is level one, presumably." She laughed. She had noticed the yellow haze around the creature, too.

"Ripper," The farmer called him." said Morgus, "The wolf." They both drew their weapons in unison as the wolf crept inexorably closer to the unsuspecting sheep.

"Come on!" he shouted. It's time for a scrap!" They both ran towards the sheep and as they did so, Morgus remembered her bow. She put her small dagger back in its hilt and held the bow instead. Pulling an arrow from the quiver, she fired an arrow at the advancing creature. The arrow shot through the air and missed the wolf completely.

Laughing loudly, Tom reached the wolf and struck it with his sword. The creature turned to face him, snapping its jaws as it did so. Every time he struck it, the creature yelped, and when it barked back at him and struck out, black lines appeared at the edge of his sight. The creature seemed to be flagging, however, and as Morgus arrived, she struck it on the back with her dagger, and the beast whimpered and lay still.

"Was there a blue flash, then?" she asked as the creature faded from view and disappeared altogether.

"We get experience points for killing the wolf," he said. "They accumulate, which allows you to grow in the things you can do."

"Advancing levels." She nodded. "I seem to remember the bit in the manual that dealt with that," she said.

"You said you never read it." He smiled, and they set off once again to collect another sheep. Once that was done and the creatures were placed in their pen, the shepherd appeared once again and passed them both a small leather bag, which jangled when they shook it. The edge of their sight flashed blue once again.

"I thank thee both with all of my heart," said the herder. Here is a pouch to keep your gold in. Tie it to your belt and keep it safe. Watch out for cutpurses in the city, too. Many a purse snatched there, it's said."

"Thank you," they replied and walked back down the hill to Pip's cabin, fastening the coin bags to their belts as they walked.

"I think this place is best experienced with a companion." she said, "How about it?"

"Sounds cool," said Tom. If that suits you, I will be back online in about ten hours." She did a calculation in her head and nodded. They reached the cabin and walked inside. The smell of cooking filled the air. The cabin was small but cosy, with a stone-lined fire on one wall and two doors leading into further rooms that were both currently closed. Astride the roaring fire was a large cooking pot from which the smell was wafting.

"I made a stew," said Pip, standing by the fire and stirring the broth. "Apologies for the heat of the fire, but it grows cold overnight, and I am prone to suffer at the hands of drafts and what have you, so I like to keep the house warm."

"I will see you later, Morgus." smiled Tom.

"I think it's probably best if you call me Susan." she smiled in embarrassment.

"That your real name?"

"It is, yes."

"Okay. Thanks for sharing that with me," he smiled. "I will see you later, Susan." He looked around him one last time, gave her a wink and said, "Log out, Avalon." There was a shimmer in the air, and he was gone.

"Taste?" said Pip, sipping from a spoon he had been stirring at the broth with. She shook her head and gave the logout command, and the world shimmered and changed around her.

There was a second of disorientation as Susan blinked. The inside of her front room came back into focus as the neural interface and the Avalon game shut down. She was lying on her couch at home once again. She had thought it best to lie down in case of dizziness the game might create.

"Please wait for a moment," said a voice from the headset. "There will be a brief moment of disorientation. This will soon pass." She closed her eyes, took a deep breath, and tilted herself forward to move from a horizontal to a vertical position. She tentatively raised her hand in front of her, focusing on it as she moved it. She sighed as the neural net released her, the feeling of her body returning to her as the game world's ease of movement faded. She was startled slightly as the house phone speakers rang, and she nodded to the screen as the call was connected.

"Miss Harker?" asked a male voice, and she affirmed that it was her.

"My name is Rod, and I am calling from the Avalon Total Immersion Company to ensure that your first experience of our simulation was a good one."

"It is amazing," she said, smiling at the fresh-faced man on her video screen on the wall, his face full of enthusiasm.

"It is really, isn't it?" he said. "Just a cursory check that everything proceeded as it should. We don't call after every use of the experience, but we will call occasionally to ensure everything is okay."

"It's fine," she said. She felt tired and hungry now, and after dismissing the call after a few more brief pleasantries, she began to think of ordering some real food—the sort with calories in it—real calories. As she did so, she thought of her Avalon avatar's appearance and looked up at the mirror on the wall.

She smiled. *The Avalon version of me is perfect—one hundred per cent better than the real me.*

She removed the headset and placed it on the bed beside her. She was tempted to go back online but resisted the urge, remembering that she was both hungry and tired. After a few minutes of pondering how the game world had felt so real, she drifted away, lost in thought, and sat staring out the window across the city's lights. *Food can wait*, she thought. Just a few more minutes of daydreaming and then sleep. She surrendered to it gratefully when it came, and dreams took her quickly.

Tom picked up the game manual and threw himself into the chair, his bathrobe floating about him as he sat. He leafed through ten pages, remembering the customer assurance call he had fielded thirty minutes ago. He considered the whole Avalon experience really to be a slick one. Not just that, of course, but it was amazing. Completely real.

He wandered through to the small kitchen and made a light sandwich. He was not one for late-night snacks, but he felt starving. He wondered for a time if the simulation did that to you? If it could? He smiled. He would have to stop thinking of it as a "simulation". It was a GAME. A very realistic game, of course, and using technology that had taken decades to perfect, but a game it most definitely was. The scenario was all there. The swords and leather armour, the shepherd and the woodcutter. It all fitted in the fantasy environment. He just couldn't wait to see what the game threw at him next, and as he did so, he thought about his brief trip there and the woman he had encountered. Morgus. No. Susan. He laughed aloud. George, more likely. Still, having a companion to play the game with would be helpful. The manual stressed it. In fact, certain areas of the game were inaccessible without the cooperation of other players.

Still. George. He laughed and threw the manual onto the floor. It was time to sleep.

She walked around the side of the cabin to see Tom was chopping logs. There were a disappointing number of logs on the floor, she noted.

"Want to try some?" asked Pip, holding out a spoon to her as Susan found herself in the woodcutter's lodge once again. She blinked, the room full of smoke, the air warm.

"It's a little early for me." she smiled. "I will have a taste later."

"Very well," said Pip, trying his best to keep the disappointment out of his voice and failing to do so completely. She looked around the room. It looked like they were both alone.

"Has the man who was with me yesterday logged on yet?" she asked, and Pip smiled and nodded.

"Tom said to tell you he is outside cutting wood for exercise until you arrive."

"Ah," she said, taking a tentative step forward. At first, she moved awkwardly to the door, but as she stepped outside into the blaze of the setting sun, she was moving naturally again. The acclimatisation process this time had been much shorter. She walked around the side of the cabin to see Tom was chopping logs. He waved as he saw her and buried the axe into the nearest log. There were a disappointing number of logs on the floor, she noted.

"How long have you been at that, then?" she asked, and he laughed. She noticed he was slightly out of breath.

"Not long. I guess I must be out of practice."

"Somehow, I don't think that Pip is going to see you as a challenge." she laughed, and Tom laughed along with her. "I see night draws in."

"Yes," he said. "The cycle of day and night is much shorter here, I seem to remember reading, but some things only happen at night and vice versa."

"Makes sense," she nodded. "So. What do we do now?"

"So far, we have sorted the shepherd out and got the wolf. No doubt there are other tasks available to us, though I suspect we start with Pip. This is just the nursery of the game. I think he will have some more things to tell us before we can move forward.

"Okay." she said, "Let's go have some stew."

"Virtual stew, hopefully, is completely free of calories." she smiled, and they both walked back into the cabin.

"Ah. Here you are," said Pip, "Food to spare I have, and make no mistake. Tasty, too. Who wants some?" They both put up a hand and sat at the table as Pip served them piping hot bowls of what looked suspiciously like a lamb stew, served with small loaves of thick, crusty white bread. Tom dug into his food, amazed at just how tasty it was. Across the table, Susan's eyebrows rose.

"You make a nice stew, Pip," she said. "This is wonderful."

"Plenty to go around if you want more," said the woodcutter.

"What are the herbs in it?" Tom asked. I just can't quite place the taste."

"It's a plain type of rosemary. It grows in the meadows below. I need some more to make my next stew. If you like, you can gather them from the meadows north of here in the morning. I need eight bunches."

"Very well," said Tom. "That's another quest we have." he said to Susan, "He probably has a few more."

"Of course, while you are there, you can see if there are any long-leafed summer flowers growing on the banks of the river. Always adds flavour to the bread, that does,"

"Told you!" smiled Tom.

"Though keep an eye out for Snapper, the wild otter that lives there. Guards his territory well, he does. Bring me his tail, and I would be mighty grateful."

"I am sure we can help," said Susan. Outside, it was dark already, and through the small cabin windows, they could see a full moon rising high across the hill.

"So where do we travel after here?" asked Tom. Pip took a pipe from the fireplace and lit it with a long taper.

"I don't think you're quite ready for the rest of Southmere just yet," he laughed. "Do those tasks for me in the morning, and we shall see what comes after that."

"Very well." said Susan, "But just for the record, where exactly are we? When you first said hello, you said that we are in Spindlebark, the southernmost province of…"

"Southmere," said Pip.

"Yes. Southmere. So where is that in terms of everywhere else?" Pip stopped to consider his reply as if he was mapping it out in his head.

"Now let me see." Pip paused and rubbed his chin as if gathering his thoughts. Tom smiled. The simulation of a real person really was quite remarkable. "Where we are now really is known as Pip's acre. Directly north is the basket of the county if you like, and that is called Puddleswat."

'Puddleswat?" laughed Susan, and Pip nodded.

"Aye. named after mayor Erastus Puddleswat, the founder of the farming practices hereabouts. He has a statue in Havenholme town square that is well worth a visit, I am told. The town is the centre of the county, at the heart of which stands the Traveller's Rest Inn, which serves the finest dark ale in all of Southmere apparently, though I have never tasted it myself. North and east of there are the South Wilds, and beyond that lie the cold stone hills of the Mence, all flint and poor soil. Not much farming is done down that way, I am sure. Beyond the Mence and the South Wilds lies The Downs, a cold and misty place to cross, but if you avoid the southernmost reaches of Tanglefoot forest, then Havenholme is to the north of there.

"Seems quite a way," said Tom. Pip laughed, blowing smoke from his pipe. Tom was amazed that the smoke was not in rings.

"That is just Southmere." he laughed, "Northmere beyond that is bigger again, and beyond that, the wilds of Avalon await. More lands north of there, too, though best not to speak of them when the moon is full. Dark places, so tales say. It is a big land. As you will see."

"Havenholme is a busy town then?" asked Susan, and Pip nodded. "Lots of adventurers make their way there to begin with. They say it is a good place to use as a base to explore the other areas of the county. Plenty of trade there, too."

"What's it like?" asked Tom.

"Like?" said Pip, as if he had misunderstood the question.

"Yes." said Tom, "Lots of buildings? More than one pub?"

"I don't know," said Pip. "I imagine so."

"Why don't you know?" smiled Susan.

"I have never been," said Pip, matter-of-factly.

"Why ever not?" laughed Susan.

"Oh, I just stay here and chop the logs and serve the stew," said Pip simply, knocking his pipe out on a bowl on the fireplace and laying it down. "Anyone want any more to eat?"

"I'm fine, thanks," said Tom and Susan shook her head.

"What would happen if I asked you to come with us to Havenholme?" asked Susan, and Pip frowned.

"Who would guide the new adventures then, Miss Susan? Who would make the stew and cut the logs? The world's a big place, I think, but I am a small part of it. I do have to say that I am content with my lot. I cannot leave here. My heart is here, really. And there are always tasks to perform. New adventurers to point in the right direction."

"I see," said Tom, and they all settled into a short silence. Pip walked to one of the doors at the back of the cabin.

"I will sleep now." he said, "Goodnight." Before either of them had a chance to respond, the little man walked into the room and closed the door behind him.

"Have we upset him?" asked Susan and Tom laughed loudly.

"He's not real, you know!" he said, "All of his responses are pre-scripted."

"I know," she said, "But it's this place…" She tapped the table and looked at the flames in the fire. "It is just so real. Everything fits to the smallest detail—the smells, the sounds, everything."

"It is pretty special," he said. They settled into an easy silence, watching the flames in the fire. They drifted away, thinking about the game they found themselves in until Susan startled and rose to her feet. Outside the cabin window, the sun was beginning to rise.

"Did we just fall asleep?" Susan asked incredulously. "Tell me that we didn't."

"I don't think so," said Tom. "I know that the day and night cycle are much quicker here, apparently."

“That was minutes,” she said, though there was an air of indecision in her voice. “Wasn’t it?”

To their consternation, Pip came in from outside carrying more logs and placed them in the fireplace's meagre ashes.

“Soon have this lot burning.” he said, “Breakfast will be about forty minutes. If I were you two, I would get down to the meadow and get those long-leafed summer flowers. Purple heads, they have. The meadow rosemary is, of course, pink. Watch out for that otter, though!”

“Which way?” smiled Susan, patting the dagger at her side.

“North.” smiled Pip. You will know that you are in the right place when you see the river. I wouldn’t cross its banks just yet, though. Just sort out the flowers and keep an eye open for Snapper, though. Nasty disposition, that otter. Never plays fair, either. Watch out for his tail.”

An hour later, they stood on the bank of a fast-flowing river beside the fading and very dead body of Snapper. The fight had been much longer than that against Ripper, the wolf, and Susan had managed to land several arrows in the Otter before it reached them, much to her delight, but this time, the creature had fought back, and as it struck at them, the periphery of their vision flashed black as they were attacked. Susan found her vision fraying around the edges, and red flashes were at the corner of her eye, but once the fight was over, she sat for a minute, and they soon faded.

“It’s how the game lets us know how the fight is going.” Said Tom. “Once your health is gone, then you have died, and the game moves you to a safe place, and the creature has won.”

“I thought as much.” Said Susan. “The game pretty much leads you by the nose, doesn’t it?”

“The way Pip needed herbs and the sheep yesterday – yes, I guess it does. Certainly at this starting area, anyway. I imagine once we begin to travel further, it will open up a lot more.”

The river flowed east to west, and to the east, it rounded a tall tree-covered hill, the river vanishing from sight as it did so.

“How long have we been gone?” she asked, and Tom shrugged.

"It's a silly idea that the game doesn't allow you to wear a watch," she said.

"I think they want you to learn to tell the time from the position of the sun. Or the moon, come to think of it."

"Probably thirty minutes or so if the daytime runs at the same time as normal time."

"Unlike the night," he said.

"Yes." she agreed. "Let's take a little walk further along the river and then head back before these flowers and herbs start to wilt. I am curious to see what lies around the river bend."

"Okay," he said, and they walked along the bank of the river, keeping a careful eye on the north bank and paying heed to Pip's warning. As they rounded the bend, they saw that the curve in the river created a central ford, several stones spanning its width. That was not what caught their attention, however, for in a small meadow very similar to the one in which they were currently standing was a tall stone tower. It was approximately thirty feet in height and had been concealed from view by the hill and the thick growth of trees that rose above it. Now, however, it stood in the sunlight, the sun breaking on the cold granite walls of the building.

"No windows or doors," said Susan.

"Not on this side, no. There may be on the other side."

"We could go and look," she said.

"Pip said not to cross the river yet. I think we don't have enough experience under our belts."

"Aw, come on!" she laughed, "Adventurers, aren't we?" Tom laughed, and they made their way to the ford and leapt from rock to rock, crossing the fast-flowing river easily. They were soon both stood on the north bank of the river. The tower was no more than three hundred feet away in the centre of a bright, clear meadow. Without consultation, both of them drew their weapons and scoured the meadow for any signs of movement at all. They could see nothing.

"Quick scout of the tower, and back we go," said Tom, and they walked quickly towards the tall stone tower. Once they reached it, they walked around its base, disappointed to find that there were neither windows nor doors to be seen anywhere.

"Strange building," muttered Tom, running his fingers across the cold granite as he did so. "I wonder what it's for?" He rapped his knuckles against the hard granite walls. Nearby, the river gurgled loudly as it cut its way across the valley. "What use is a building with no way to get inside it?"

"Tom," said Susan, tension in her voice. "We got a problem." Tom spun on his heels to see a large black bear heading their way, roaring as it raced towards them. As they looked at it, a small purple aura appeared above the creature's head, and then it faded.

"Purple." He gulped. "It's a much higher level than us!" shouted Tom. "Run!"

They raced from the tower, but the bear was surprisingly fast, and it flanked them easily and then tore towards them, its sharp claws swinging towards them as it reared up on its hind legs, rising above them. Susan thrust forward with her dagger, but the creature swung at her and threw her through the air. There was a small black popping sound in her ears, and she vanished. Tom thrust his sword at the bear and saw it flinch, and then its deadly assault fell upon him. The periphery of his vision exploded in black, and the bear vanished. Slowly, his eyes re-focused, and he was sitting next to Susan on the south bank of the river again.

"So that's what it's like to be killed in the game," laughed Susan.

"Yes. I just think that we shall leave the bears for now." He stood, and as she held her hand out to him, he helped her to her feet.

"Still. That tower is a bit of a mystery, isn't it?"

"It is," he said. "I think the game is slowly sucking us in. We will be addicts at this rate."

"Easily done, I think. Already, I have no idea how long I have been online."

"Time is difficult to work out, though," he said. "For what it's worth, I think no more than two hours." Susan frowned. "It's just that there is so much packed into that time that it seems longer. I suppose the game has to do it to keep your attention. If it was all stew and sleeping, then you may as well stay sat in your own armchair." Susan laughed.

"The stew was nice, though."

"It was. Very nice indeed." He looked in his bag and saw the flowers and rosemary. "Come on - let's get these back to Pip. We may gain enough experience credit to go and kick some bear's ass."

Laughing, they wandered back across the meadow towards Pip's cabin. As they did so, Tom pointed out a path leading down the hill towards the building at the edge of the fields. Small stone walls rose on each side of the path as it meandered through the fields towards the cabin. It disappeared across the meadows to the northeast.

"It's the road," said Tom. We will need to have a look at that at some point I would have thought. They glanced at the road, and as they did so, a small cart came into view heading down the hill towards Pip's cabin.

They stopped to mark its progress down the lane, for it was not moving quickly, but the road was on the other side of the meadow, and the stone walls were relatively high, so it was difficult to keep track of. Nevertheless, as it drew closer, they could see that it was a small, flat-backed wagon pulled by a single brown horse. At the reins sat a stooped man covered in a long grey cloak. Upon his head, he wore a pointed hat with a wide brim that drooped wearily about his head. As they walked nearer to the cart, almost running across the meadow to get a closer look, they saw a long white beard jutting from under the hat. The man smoked a small pipe and blew small plumes of smoke into the air as he drove along, the smoke following behind the cart before fading idly in the warm mid-morning air.

"Looks like Pip has a visitor," said Tom as the cart reached the cabin and out strode Pip. hands on hips. Ton and Susan were both quite close to the cabin now but not close enough to be able to hear what it was that Pip said, but after he had said it, he stormed back into his house and slammed the door firmly shut behind him. Undeterred, the old man climbed slowly down from the cart and supported himself with a long wooden staff that was almost as tall as he was. He stood on the doorstep, banging on the door with the staff.

"Oh, come now, Pip!" the old man shouted almost wearily, "Don't be like this. Open the door and let me in. I cannot stand on your doorstep all day. Unlock the door and let me in!"

"with a stamp of his foot
he scratched a large cross
on the door with his staff."

"Go away!" they heard Pip shout from inside the cabin. "I have told you more than once. You are not wanted around here, what with all of your talk of adventures and nonsense. I have logs to chop and stew to make. Be on your way, Garoch! I will not waste a single breath listening to your silly words! Begone!"

The old man turned to look at Tom and Susan as they reached the house. He grinned at them as if in embarrassment.

"Locked me out," he said, banging on the door again with his staff. "Bit awkward, really. Still. I am sure that he will reconsider."

"I see," Susan said. The man looked them up and down again, suddenly surprised.

"I don't suppose you have a key, do you?" he said, and they both shook their heads.

"Only for the small cabin at the bottom of the path."

"By the well?" asked Garoch, pointing his staff at the small white building.

"Yes."

"Ah." he said, "Not much use, I am afraid." He redoubled his assault on the door with his staff, shouting loudly as he did so. "Do not make me angry now, Pip." he roared, "I am knocking on this door entirely out of politeness. I am a very busy man and have little time for nonsense such as this." There was still silence. "Open the door!" the old man roared, but from inside, nothing could now be heard at all.

"Damned fool," muttered Garoch under his breath, and with a stamp of his foot, he scratched a large cross on the door with his staff. "There," he muttered to nobody in particular. "That's done, and that's all there is to it. Serves him right too, if you ask me." He stood back from the door.

"I'm pleased to meet you both," he smiled, tipping the brim of his hat. Without further ado, he walked back to his cart and, slowly and carefully turning it around, drove it away in the direction that he had just come from.

"What was that all about?" asked Susan.

"No idea," said Tom, "No idea at all."

As they stood looking at the cross on the door, they heard a key turning in the lock from within the hut. Slowly, the door edged open a little. Through the crack, they looked down and saw the diminutive figure of Pip looking up at them.

"Has he gone?" he asked, and Susan nodded. With a sigh, Pip opened the door, and they went inside.

"What did he want?" asked Tom. Pip threw himself down into a chair and sat, head in his hands.

"Just won't leave me alone." he sighed, "Wants to send me off on adventures and what have you and won't take no for an answer. But who would make the stew and show the new arrivals around if good old Pip was not here, I say?"

"He left a big mark on your door," Susan said, and Pip rose wearily from the chair and fetched a bucket and a cloth.

"Yes. He always does that. I just clean it off again. Not that it matters. Even if I left it there, it doesn't actually do anything."

They watched as Pip went outside, and they followed him through the window. He made his way to the well and began to draw water.

"I think that's enough for me today," said Tom. "What about you?"

"Ditto." I have a few work assignments to sort out.

"What is it you do?" asked Tom, and she smiled.

"I am a designer. Freelance. I dress up homes, shops and so on for people with far more money than sense and try to correct their overwhelmingly appalling lack of taste." Tom laughed. "What do you do?"

"Oh, this and that," he said mysteriously, and seeing the frown appear on her face, he capitulated. "I am trained as an architect. "

"Sounds glamorous."

"Believe me, it is anything but. It's a bit like your work, really."

"How so?" she asked, looking puzzled.

"I design homes, shops and so on for people with far more money than sense and try to correct their overwhelmingly appalling lack of taste," he laughed. "What time are you online tomorrow?"

"Same as today?" she asked, and he nodded.

"See you then. Logout Avalon." There was a shimmer, and she was gone.

"Logout Avalon," said Tom and the simulation melted away until his home formed around him once again, welcoming him back with its warm familiarity.

Avalon User Manual: The User Interface

Avalon (TM) is the first multiplayer fantasy Total Immersion (TM) game from Avalon Productions (TM). As such, we recommend you familiarise yourself with the game controls and read this manual carefully before venturing into the game's starter area. As we are sure you are aware, the experience of the game is quite unlike anything else available, and the technology that drives the experience is the most advanced on the market.

Avalon (TM) was created to immerse the player in the environment, and as such, it was a design must from the very start that the interface should never get in the way of the game. You will not see life points, character stats, resistances, bonuses, and so on in Avalon, as we felt it would interfere with play.

For example, you may come across a bow and a quiver of arrows in the game. Just as in real life, the first time you use the bow, you may find it challenging to use, and when you fire an arrow, it misses your target altogether. If you are lucky and hit a target, however, it will give you the confidence to try harder, and so your experience grows until the bow you are using becomes a deadly weapon in your hands. The bow now *feels* easier to use. Drawing an arrow is second nature. This is how Avalon works. At first, you will be all fingers and thumbs, but as you gain experience in a weapon – or any task- it will feel easier. Eventually, you may even become an expert!

However, the system gives a few hints as to what is happening via small flashes of light at the corner of your vision. If you gain experience in something or gain a level, then you will notice a slight blue flash in the corner of your eye. There are others. If you attack a creature, it will fight back, and if it lands a blow, you will see a small black flash at the edge of your vision. If the creature kills you, that black will cover your sight and clear once the game moves you to safety.

Sometimes, a particular food or drink will enhance your abilities in the game. A yellow flash would show this as you eat or drink them. It is usually the case that such boosts to your abilities run on a timer. When they expire, your screen will flash yellow again. Please note that it is not possible to "Stack" such items beyond the maximum allowed bonus time. (For example, if you eat a pie that grants an extra amount of strength for thirty minutes and ten minutes into that, you eat another pie, then the total boon time is still thirty minutes, not forty. The screen would flash yellow on each occasion.)

It is worth noting that when you "die" in-game, you lose a small amount of experience, meaning it will take you longer to reach the next level. Approach each situation cautiously, and if a creature is too high a level for you (higher than yellow), either wait until you have more experience or group up with fellow players to tip the odds in your favour. The more of you there are, the higher the creatures you take on can be, as is the resulting experience. Groups of players have a much better chance of bringing down a high-level creature, and the experience of doing so is shared amongst all the victors.

Therefore, it is a careful balancing act to ensure the maximum amount of experience amongst the optimal number of players. Please enjoy the game, but remember to immerse yourself slowly and take frequent breaks once you have done so. The neural headset is self-maintaining, but please use common sense when playing Avalon (TM)—it is a total immersion experience, and it will take some time to acclimatise yourself!

Have fun out there, and happy adventuring!

PART TWO

"The mark on the door has gone," said Susan as they strolled away from the hut and across the meadow towards the river.

"I noticed," said Tom. "Not a trace. Pip must have cleared it off. He said he was going to."

They had spent a few minutes handing in the wild rosemary and flowers they had gathered and forgotten all about the day before, the edges of their sight flickering blue as they did so.

"Maybe the bear is less dangerous now?" she said, and so they went down to the river to find out. If the purple flash above the bear's head was any other colour, then it would be a much more viable target.

"Could be," said Tom. "If not, we may have to run back with our tails between our legs and see if Pip has any other bits and pieces that we can help him out with to gain more experience."

"I want to fight the bear." she laughed, so they walked across the meadow and down to the crook in the stream. As they rounded the bend, they saw the bear on the far side of the river. It did not seem to have noticed them, however, and so they slowly crept a little further forward, reasoning that they were safe as they did so. They had the full width of the river between them, they thought, even if it was a ford.

"It's orange," said Susan. "What does that mean?"

"I seem to recall that the manual said purple was way too strong for us, and yellow is just above our own limit, but given luck, it is still possible to defeat it. Orange is just above yellow in the spectrum, so maybe the two of us could take it down.

"The bear looked around, gave a loud roar and began to race across the ford of the river before them."

"Let's give it a go!" she shouted, shouldering her bow and nocked an arrow. "I will get it over to us, and then we can both lay into it."

"Okay," said Tom, withdrawing his sword. "Let's do it!"

Susan fired an arrow across the stream, and it flew wide of the bear by a considerable distance. She then aimed another arrow which hit the bear on the flank. Susan gave a loud cry of delight as the bear looked around, gave a loud roar and raced across the ford of the river before them.

"Keep shooting it!" shouted Tom, bracing himself as the bear left the river behind it and raced towards them, roaring loudly as it did so. Another arrow flew towards the bear, catching it on its back this time, and as it thundered towards them, Tom threw himself at it and hit it with his sword. Instantly, the creature raised itself above him, paws swinging wildly and at the edge of his vision, black flashes sparkled as the bear attacked him.

"Forget the bow now," he shouted as he began to have to move backwards, clumsily raising his shield between him and the raking attacks of the bear. "Attack it with the dagger from behind!"

Susan ran around the bear and thrust her dagger into it. It roared and made to turn towards her, but as it was now distracted, Tom struck it with his sword several times. The bear tried to turn back to him just as Susan struck it again. It gave a final roar and collapsed to the ground. They both saw a bright blue flash of light, and the bear slowly vanished.

"Well done!" laughed Susan. "Definitely looks like two heads are better than one!"

They walked forward to the ford and sat down on the riverbank, watching the water flow past. Insects hummed in the air, and the air was redolent with the smell of meadow flowers.

"Is this where we crossed the river yesterday?" asked Susan suddenly, confusion in her voice.

"Yes. It's the only place where there seems to be a ford that I have noticed. It was here we crossed yesterday, yes."

"Then where is the tower?" she asked, and Tom looked around

the far bank, thunderstruck. The tower was not there!

"Come on!" he said, standing and running towards the ford to cross the river to the other side, "Let's go and have a look!"

They hopped across the river and walked into the meadow, heading towards where the small stone tower had stood the day before. The grass of the meadow was completely undisturbed, and there was no debris or sign at all that a tower had stood exactly where they were standing now the day before.

"It's gone," said Susan and Tom nodded.

"Not even any flattened grass or anything. Just another mystery."

'Perhaps we should ask Pip about it when we get back. He may know something about it."

"Worth a try, I suppose."

They ventured a little further north, gazing across the fields and meadows. In the distance, several haystacks were visible, but as they stood watching the horizon, they saw much nearer a larger bear than the one they had just defeated at the far end of the meadow. As they looked at it, they saw an aura of the deepest purple about it. It was still a fair distance off, so they withdrew and crossed back over the ford, wandering back towards Pip's hut.

"Not all bears are the same level then." She smiled, Tom, nodding in agreement.

As they drew nearer, they saw that the small man was standing by the well, turning the winch. He paused in his work, waved to them, and they drew closer. He pulled a full bucket from the stone circle that surrounded the waterhole and tipped it into a smaller pan that rested on the ground.

"You two weren't gone long." he smiled. "What chased you back?"

"We just came to see if you needed any help," said Tom.

"I am fine," said Pip, "Dinner will be ready in an hour, though, so you may as well come indoors." They did so and sat watching the small man prepare food, moving around the tiny kitchen with amazing speed. Outside, the sun began to set, and within ten minutes, it was dark. Pip had already lit several lanterns, so the house was brightly lit.

"That sun set early," said Susan, "Much earlier than yesterday."

"It's probably scripted," said Tom, "Means something is going to happen that needs to be done at night."

"Strange area, it is so out of sequence," she said.

"It will probably not be so jarring once we are out of the nursery area." he laughed. "For now, we must just go with the flow."

"Pip, what do you know about a tower down in the meadow?" he asked. Pip stopped stirring a pot he had been concentrating on for the last few minutes and looked blankly at them both.

"A tower?" he asked, and Susan nodded.

"About thirty feet high. Looked like granite. No doors or windows."

"Are you sure?" asked Pip, and Tom nodded his head.

"Yes. Very sure."

"I have never heard or seen sight or sound of that," said Pip. I will go and have a look at it tomorrow. If I have new neighbours, it would have been polite for them to introduce themselves."

"That's the problem, Pip." said Susan, "It's not there now. It was definitely there yesterday, but not there today."

"Strange. I don't think a tower can just disappear." laughed Pip, "Are you sure you were looking in the right place?"

"Very sure," said Tom.

"Now then, there's a mystery," said Pip and returned to stirring the pot, the tower now apparently completely forgotten.

Tom raised an eyebrow, and Susan smiled at him. Shortly after, the food was served.

"Pan-fried fish from the river with a stew of vegetables and home-grown potatoes," said Pip as he handed out generously laden plates of food. He pulled a chair up to the table and clambered up into it, joining them for the meal. There was silence as the first mouthfuls were eaten, and Pip poured three glasses of clear white liquid from a small clay jar that stood in the centre of the table.

"Wine?" asked Tom, and Pip nodded.

"It's lovely," said Susan, taking a larger sip than her first tasting.

"The fish is cooked to perfection, too."

"Thank you." smiled Pip, "I like to make my guests welcome, and food is the main part of that."

"What do you suggest we do next, Pip?" asked Tom, keen to see what the small man would make of his question. He looked a little puzzled at first, Tom thought, but soon he brightened up and seemed to focus on something that looked as if it had just occurred to him.

"I think that once you have crossed the river, then it's north you need to be heading. Southmere is a big place, you know, though you need to make your aim to get to Havenholme. From there, you can strike out any way that you choose."

"So, just head north?"

"Yes."

"Only we noticed a furious-looking bear in that direction, which I suspect would give us a bit of a hiding if we are not careful around it. I suspect it is not the only one as well."

"You need to stick to the riverbank at first," said Pip, "head east along the near bank and from there north and across the river."

"I think we may just try that when it gets light," said Susan as she continued to eat. "We can just sneak around the bears?"

"You could try," smiled Pip. "Though you need to reach the haystacks in the fields to the north. Beyond that are a few more fields. One is more important than others."

"Why?" asked Tom, putting down his knife and fork.

"It's the only way to get to Puddleswat." smiled Pip. "that's the next area to the north. It's the first step in your approach to Havenholme, really. Just try one step at a time."

"So what are we looking for?" asked Susan, "To get to Puddleswat. Is it a gate or a road, or what?"

"More of a portal," said Pip, smiling. It is one way, though. Once you are through there, you cannot return. You will be out in the big old wide world on your own, then. No Pip to hold your hand." The man chuckled and rose to a small cupboard at the side of the room. Opening the draw, he pulled out two identical small scrolls.

He passed one to Tom and the other to Susan.

"Here." he said, "look at that."

Curious, Tom opened the scroll, and Susan did the same. Pip looked over their shoulders and pointed out the route on the map.

"If you go past the haystacks and into the fields beyond, you will see tall cliffs blocking your way north. Before them are small clumps of trees. If you look for the clearing in the circle on the map a circular portal is behind the northernmost tree."

"It sounds as if it could be a little perilous."

"It is, yes." smiled Pip, "But there is nothing that benefits that is given freely. If you take care, you will see the portal. Once you discover it, you will gain a great deal of experience. That would mean if you wished, you could stay and conduct a bear hunt before you left via the portal, which would have the benefit of giving you even more points. It is up to you, really. Some are keen to progress onwards, some less so. It makes little difference to me."

Tom folded up the map and placed the scroll in his bag. Outside, he saw it was still dark.

"I take it that such a journey would be much more perilous at night?" smiled Susan, and Pip looked troubled at the suggestion.

"You will find, Susan and Tom, that the roads of Avalon are always much more dangerous of a night. Bears would be the least of your troubles were you to take that road under cover of darkness. There are many things in the wide world, and we must not be careless to assume that we know what they all are."

"I see." said Susan, "That is us told then."

"So you advise waiting until morning?" asked Tom, and Pip nodded.

"It makes much more sense." said Pip, "Besides. I have a nice apple tart in the oven. More wine, anyone?"

They both agreed that another drink was an excellent proposition and settled back in their seats to relax. As they did so they both shot into the air as a sudden loud knock came on the door. They leapt to their feet as the knock came again. It sounded like a heavy club was being struck against the wood!

"Open up!" shouted a familiar, deep voice. "In the name of all that is precious to you, let me in! There are strange creatures on the road, and I think they may have followed me!"

"Garoch," said Pip in a deflated fashion. He rose and went to the door. But he did not open it.

"Begone, wizard!" he shouted, "I have told you many times. Do not darken my doorstep again!"

"Let me in, you fool!" shouted the old man, "This is not a ploy to get you to allow me entry. I am in danger out here! Quickly! Open the door!"

"Go away!" shouted Pip angrily, and Tom walked over to the door.

"Pip." he said, placing a hand on the short man's shoulder, "I think we should let him in. He genuinely sounds afraid."

"Listen to him, I beg you!" shouted Garoch from outside, "He talks sense! There are creatures out here, the likes of which I have never seen before! Let me in! I am convinced they are hot on my tail!"

"Never!" shouted Pip as Susan came to where Pip stood, his back to the door, his teeth gritted. Tom stood beside him, a look of exasperation on his face.

"How many times has Garoch come to try and get in of a night, Pip?" she asked, and the small man gave her a look of dismissal but then seemed to think about it a little longer.

"Actually, never." he frowned.

"It is always daylight when he comes, then?" she asked, kneeling down beside him.

"Always, yes."

"Yet now it is night."

"Yes, it is.

"I think we need to let him in, Pip. There is something different about his behaviour this night if he always normally comes in the day."

"Let me in!" shouted Garoch. "I think something draws near!"

Pip sighed and stood away from the door. Tom turned the key in the lock and threw the door wide. The man outside did not hesitate, throwing himself across the threshold. Tom glanced out into the darkness outside, but he saw nothing. From nearby, however, came a slight buzzing sound, and a small bolt of blue lightning forked into the ground, revealing the meadow momentarily before it disappeared into darkness once again, the brief impression of it burning into his eyes. Tom frowned and threw the door shut, turning the key in the lock.

"Did you see anything?" asked Garoch, grabbing Tom by the shoulders and staring at him, fear written on his face. He was dressed exactly how he had been the previous day: long grey cloak and pointed, wide-brimmed hat of the same colour. He still carried his long wooden staff, which he was leaning on heavily, clearly out of breath. He looked terrified.

"I saw a fork of lightning in the meadow," said Tom.

"Was it blue?" Garoch spat at him, his grip on Tom's shoulders even harder.

"Yes. It was."

"That was it." he said, "I was heading south of The Mence towards Puddleswat with the idea of camping in The Downs before setting out to arrive here in the morning."

'No doubt with the aim of trying to get me to embark on some ridiculous adventure or another, ' said Pip angrily. Have a mind, wizard. Were it not for these two fair folks taking pity on you, then you would still be on the other side of my door.'

"Then that would leave me in great peril." said Garoch, "For as dusk began to fall and I searched the lower hills of Puddleswat for a suitable camping site, I began to hear stirrings in the woods."

"Bandits, no doubt," said Pip, "I have always been told that bandits are no match for a wizard of the north. Could it be I wonder that I was misinformed?"

"Not at all." sniffed Garoch testily, "Many a bandit has looked in despair upon my visage as the last thing that they shall ever see in their miserable thieving life. This, however, was no bandit or brigand eager to relieve an old man of his wares. No. This was the stuff of nightmares. At first all I could hear was a sound like wood burning, and then as dusk crept across the fields, I could see in the near distance blue flashes of light and lightning, then further off to the west the same."

"You think there were several of whatever it was that pursued you?" asked Susan, and Garoch nodded in agreement. From outside the cabin, the sound of a horse whinnying in fear could be heard.

"Indeed. At least three. What they are, I cannot tell. I have never seen their like before, but they call to each other, a whining sound that is speech, I am sure, but too coarse for my ear to interpret."

"So, you fled here with them following you?"

"Yes." said Garoch, "It was the only place that I thought I could reach before they caught up with me. It was a furious flight from Puddleswat, but I made it. Just."

"Well, this is exciting," said Susan, patting Tom on his back. She was startled to note that he felt excited, too. "You were right about the reason night fell so quickly."

"It looks like it," said Tom. Would you like to continue this tomorrow night, though? I am not sure that I have enough time for this today. I have a few projects I need to pick up on for work."

"Sure," said Susan. "It will just carry on from where we left it. Same time tomorrow?"

"Sounds good," said Tom. "Try to free up a few more hours, and I will do the same. I think the next part of the game may take a little while."

"I think you're right. I'll free up a few more hours then. See you tomorrow."

"Have a good day," he said, and she smiled.

"You too." She looked at Garoch, staring at Pip, who was looking angrier by the second, and chuckled to herself. "Log out, Avalon," she said.

Nothing happened.

"Tom," she said just as he gave the same logout command. He looked shocked as nothing happened to him either. "The logout command isn't working."

"Impossible," he said. "The game cannot keep you online against your will. It's against every security protocol that the industry has put in place before granting a licence to build even just one neural headset." Through the window, he saw a blue fork of lightning illuminate the meadow and then vanish. It was much closer now. 'Logout Avalon." he said. Still, nothing happened.

"Logout Avalon," said Susan, the command having exactly the same result as before. Nothing happened at all.

"Something is obviously wrong with the system," said Tom. "I am sure there are systems in place that will deal with such an eventuality. All we have to do is sit tight and wait for them to fix the problem."

"I hope it doesn't take them long," said Susan, "Though it's not good, is it?"

"Not good at all," said Tom. Garoch walked to the centre of the room and placed his staff against the table, stopping midstep and turning to face them both. Pip remained with his back to the door, a perfect picture of fright. Garoch, however, had stopped moving altogether. Even his breathing seemed to cease.

"Garoch?" asked Tom, waving one hand in front of the wizard's face. He did not even blink. Suddenly a bright white beam of light appeared from Garoch's eyes, widening as it hit the floor. Tom and Susan stood back, and a face appeared in the light, staring at them. The face was that of a young man, probably in his mid-twenties. He looked slightly confused but also vaguely worried and was trying very hard not to show it. Strangely, he was not dressed in a style from the game. In fact, his black T-shirt could clearly be seen to have the large word "NERDY AND PROUD" printed in large block capitals on it.

"Sorry about the inconvenience," said the man in a strong South Wales accent, "Dylan here from second-line technical support. We are aware of the issue with the logout procedures and are working on a solution. Would you like a ticket number?"

"I just want to log out, please," said Tom through gritted teeth.

"Yes. Well. We are looking at that. We are having difficulty in establishing why you are still online, you see. Everyone else has been kicked out of the game - thrown offline I mean, sorry.

"What? Every player?" said Susan. Dylan gave what he obviously thought was a comforting smile that failed to reassure them in any way whatsoever.

"Well. As far as we can tell, anyway. We are actually locked out ourselves at the moment. Still, I am sure we will be able to get you back soon instead of having to use this backdoor through one of the development tools. It has limited use, you see. Still, bear with us. All will be fine soon."

"So what do we do in the meantime?" asked Susan, and Dylan looked vaguely startled.

"There are two of you?" he asked. Susan nodded.

"Yes. Of course, there are."

"Oh," said Dylan. "Right-ho. Well, I am sure we can get it all sorted soon. As I say. Just bear with us."

"So, shall we just carry on with the game for now?"

"If you want," said Dylan brightly. "No reason not to. May help pass the time, I suppose."

"We are under attack by strange forks of lightning at the moment." laughed Tom. "All we have had so far is a wolf and a bear. Quite a change."

In the projected image, Dylan's expression suddenly changes, his mouth forming a perfect "O".

"Blue lightning, by any chance?" he asked innocently.

"Yes. Just that so far."

"Right-oh," said Dylan. "Hang on a minute, please." The light vanished suddenly, but Garoch remained frozen. Tom looked at Susan and arched an eyebrow.

"Log out, Avalon," she said. Still, nothing happened. Suddenly, the beam of light reappeared, and Dylan was back.

"Now, I don't want to panic you," said Dylan. But we are pretty much in agreement that you need to get as far away from those little bursts of lightning as you can."

"Why?" asked Susan.

"It would seem – as far as we can make out, anyway - that they are sort of like anti-virus programs in layman's terms," said Dylan, "Which means that they can override some of the core program parameters. What we can't understand at the moment is why they are there and why they are attacking you. They can't actually do that. You see. Bit of a problem they are proving to be."

"Hang on," said Susan. Are you saying that they could actually hurt us? I mean, like, physically hurt us?" Dylan gulped but said nothing. Jesus," she said, "Your company is in serious trouble if you are telling me what I think you are telling me."

"We are pretty sure that they are unlikely to kill you as such," said Dylan. "Well. We had a right old argument about it, actually. Well, the possibility of it. We didn't know it was going to happen. Divided tech support right down the middle that discussion did, I can tell you. Rupert from Customer Liaison looked as if he was going to explode, so he did. Haven't seen him that angry since they cancelled "Firefly". Bit of a rumpus, all in all."

"What was the final verdict?" asked Susan, and Dylan gulped again.

"Well, it certainly had potential," said Dylan. "Just needed a bit of a cash injection and reassurance to the showrunner, really. Good cast, I do have to say, like." He paused briefly, noting the mounting look of anger on Susan and Tom's faces. "Oh. You didn't mean "Firefly", did you? Right. If I were you, then I would keep out of its way." he said, "We have another development tool at Havenholme. Once we disconnect here, this one is done with. We have done what we could, though. The truth is, Pip's just there to say hello, really. We will upgrade him a bit to help you out. Garoch's okay, what with him being a wizard and all. Just make sure he steers clear of the old fire water, though. Gets a bit unreasonable when pissed he does."

"So it's just the blue virus thing we have to keep away from?" said Tom, a scowl on his face. Dylan looked more than a little out of his depth.

"I would play it safe with most things, really," he said eventually.

"It looks like the part of the program that limits real-time damage isn't quite working as it should. Tried everything to get it back up and running we have, but it's just not having it."

"Are you telling me you are leaving us to get on with this with a killer virus on the loose, the entire game wanting to kill us - and kill us for real - and the ability to log out of the game removed?" said Susan, anger growing on her face.

"I agree it's a bit of a bugger. Though it's not a virus as such." He paused, rubbing his chin. "In fact, we're not quite sure what it is." He smiled weakly, "But we have limited time here. Get to Havenholme. We can probably get you out from there. Get you offline, so to speak. Ask for Charlie at the Inn."

"Never mind, "Ask for Charlie at the Inn"!" shouted Susan, "I am going to sue your collective asses off when I get out of here!"

"Sorry." said Dylan, "But the connection is fading. Remember. Keep out of that blue lightning's way and head for Havenholme. Oh, and watch out for the barr…"

The light faded to a small square. "Please rate your customer service call from one through four, where four is "excellent", and one is "needs attention". The Avalon (TM) Total Immersion Company thanks you for your business. Your ticket number is 1697023."

"I'll bloody rate you!" shouted Tom, but the light swiftly vanished as Garoch picked his staff back up and walked back to the door as if nothing had happened. Pip stood motionless, his head trembling slightly as if he was having a very fast conversation with someone that only he could hear. Suddenly, his eyes opened wide, and he stood back from the door.

"Right!" he said, "Let's get this cart outside moving. We have got some serious arse-kicking to do!" Garoch stood open-mouthed as the newly upgraded Pip kicked a carpet out from under his feet and raised a small trapdoor open. He rummaged around in the hole underneath for a moment and then lifted out a small, evil-looking black metal sword and a round shield. He strapped the shield to his arm and placed the sword in the hilt of a belt that he had just taken from the hidden stash.

"Are you perfectly alright, dear fellow?" asked Garoch, and Pip winked in reply.

"Looks like they kept their word on upgrading Pip then." Said Tom, and Susan nodded, anger still showing on her face.

"Never felt better." Said Pip. "We need to get these two to Havenholme, which means we need to escape the blue creatures you seem to have led to my door."

"I had no choice!" said Garoch angrily, but Pip waved away his protests.

"I know that, and now is no time to argue. We have to move, and we have to move quickly. These two have never been to Puddleswat, so they need to use the portal, as do I. You can go directly, Garoch."

"I think it is best that I stay with you all." said the wizard, "Safety in numbers and all that. I do believe that I have been given the charge to ensure that you both make it alive to Havenholme. The roads are dangerous, and many perils await those who stray from the path. I shall be your guide and protect you from harm as we cross the southern edge of Southmere."

"Excellent," said Pip as Tom and Susan stood watching him with expressions of shock on their faces. The change in the little man was amazing! "Garoch and I will sit up on the running board of the cart outside. Garoch, I will drive. You be ready with your staff. The wizard nodded but said nothing. "Tom. Susan. Once the cart starts to move, run and throw yourselves on the back of it. Keep your heads down below the railings, and do not try to sit up. Hold onto anything you can. We shall not be sparing the horse, I am afraid."

"Okay," said Tom, and Susan nodded, looking to Tom for reassurance. He remained tight-lipped but nodded his head in agreement. She stretched her legs, ready to do as Pip had asked.

Ready, Garoch?" asked Pip, and the wizard nodded. Pip flung open the door, and Garoch ran outside, his staff raised before him. Tom stood behind Susan as Pip vanished through the door.

Through the window, they saw him leap up onto the cart's running board and take the reins. From outside, they also saw a flash of blue lightning crash across the meadow near hand.

"Now!" shouted Pip from outside, and Tom and Susan raced from the house. The cart began to move away down the path. Susan sprinted and threw herself onto the flatbed of the cart, twisting as she lay to watch Tom sprinting towards her, trying to do the same. As he did so, however, a bright blue flash appeared on the path behind them, and Tom tumbled to the ground, the cart moving away, gathering speed. He stood and looked up as a ball of lightning formed in front of him. He stood motionless, not heeding Susan's screams behind him.

The bright blue lightning began to form itself into human shape, a horned head, arms and legs, the detail slowly forming into that of dark black and electric blue sigiled armour. The horns on the head became a helmet, and the figure moved slightly, and a sword of blue crackling flame was in its hand. Tom drew his sword and lunged at the creature, but it battered his thrust aside easily and blue fire raced up his arm, the whole world tilting as pain made him scream. He turned, his arm useless, and his sword dropped to the ground as he raced towards the cart and, reaching it, leapt onto it, Susan grabbing him as he did so.

He lay in the cart, his mind screaming with pain as he clutched at his useless arm, the agony drowning out the night as they fled north, the cart rattling as fast as it could through the night along the narrow country lane. From the fields beyond, blue flashes of fire and screams erupted, following the cart. Susan grabbed hold of Tom and made sure he kept down. She wanted to examine his arm, but in the darkness and the swaying and bumping of the cart, she knew she would be wasting her time.

"I cannot see where we are going!" shouted Pip from the running board of the cart.

"Very well!" shouted Garoch. "I can light our way, but of course, it gives away our position!"

"I don't think those things need to be able to see us to know where we are," said Pip, "Light the way if you can, or our flight will end in disaster!"

Swaying slightly and holding onto the wooden board that separated the front of the cart from the back, Garoch held his staff high into the air, muttering quietly under his breath. As he did so, the end of the staff began to glow brightly, and as it did so, the road ahead became visible.

"Excellent!" shouted Pip, "Now, where to?"

"We need the portal from your map," said Garoch, struggling to keep his balance as the truck careered down the bumpy lane. "Both Susan, Tom and you have to leave here by that. I will follow you."

"So which way?" asked Pip, confusion in his voice. On the flatbed of the cart behind them, Susan ensured that Tom had a good grip with his good arm and then dragged herself up to the running board so she could see where they were headed.

"The map," she said. "You gave it to us, Pip. You must know the way!" Pip looked slightly embarrassed.

"I don't have any idea," he said. "I just give the map out. The truth of the matter is I have never even set foot on the other side of the river."

"But you said you would check the tower out when we told you where it was," Susan said accusingly.

"Yes. But that was just narrative. Before now, I had my own set areas I could access, and that was it." He whipped the reins as another blue flash crashed through the fields to the east, keeping pace with them easily. As if in answer, another blue flash shattered the night off to the west. "Now, however, it seems that I can go where I like. The map seems to show two groups of quite thick trees. Beyond that, there are three small clumps of bushes and a single tree just a little farther north than that. The portal is marked directly east of that single tree."

"So, we are looking first of all for two thick wooded areas before a tall cliff?" asked Garoch. Pip nodded. "This may be more difficult than you think in the dark."

"How do we cross the river?" asked Susan.

"There is a small stone bridge east of the Ford. We cross the river there," said Garoch.

"I never saw that," said Susan.

"Nor me." said Pip, "But then I wouldn't have come this far before, would I?"

"Once you are in Puddleswat, then the way backwards and forwards is obvious. That is the way I travel," said Garoch. "But the first time you enter, you have to use the portal. It is the requirements of the first narrative."

"Narrative?" asked Susan.

"Yes." said Garoch, "Pip's treasure map. Campaign Quest one. We should be at the bridge soon. I would get my head back down if I were you. The bridge is a perfect place for an ambush."

"The river was fast approaching from the west. The bridge was near…"
"

Susan slid down the wooden panel and reached for Tom who lay on the floor of the cart clutching at his arm whilst trying at the same time to make sure that he did not get bounced out of the cart altogether.

"How is it?" asked Susan.

"Really hurts." he said, "Like a sting, almost. Did you see what it looked like?"

"Yes. Scariest anti-virus program I have ever seen."

"Perhaps it takes on the attributes of its surroundings," said Tom. What I do know is that it managed to hurt me, and if we had not gotten away, then I think that might not have been the end of it."

"How many of them are there, do you think?"

"I think three." he said, "The one that confronted me lit up the surrounding fields, and it looked as if in that flash of light, I could see two others rushing towards me from both the east and the west."

"They are still there." She said, "They are keeping pace with the cart, but there is no sign of the third one."

"I think it will be at the bridge." said Tom, "It's the obvious place."

"Agreed." "Is there any other place we can cross the river other than the bridge?" she called to Pip and Garoch, who were guiding the cart along the lane at what felt like breakneck speed.

"It is much deeper and wider here." said Garoch without turning, "We would never get the cart across the water. We need the bridge."

They trundled along the lane, and Susan saw through the wooden slats that the river was fast approaching from the west. The bridge was near.

"Hold!" called Garoch, and the cart drew to a rapid stop, the horse whinnying and stamping the ground as it did so.

Susan slipped down and walked around to the front of the cart. Ahead of them was a small hump-backed stone bridge crossing over the river that raced underneath its arched back, running east and west. In the lane in front of them stood a tall figure, its shape crackling with bolts of blue energy that flowed and flickered about its blue-etched metallic armour. It stood at least seven feet tall with a long two-handed sword in its hand. A horned helm covered its head, but two bright blue circles of energy flickered about where the eyes should be. It blocked the bridge completely.

"Watch it!" shouted Tom as he appeared from the back of the cart, still holding his arm, "That thing can hurt you pretty badly. I think it may be capable of killing you, in fact."

"We shall see," said Garoch, jumping down from the running board and holding his staff towards the tall creature. There came a fierce burst of white light, and the creature roared as the force of the beam hit it, staggering backwards and growling loudly. Tom looked across to the east, seeing another blue ball of flame heading rapidly towards them as fast as it could cover the distance.

The blue man raised his sword and swung it at the wizard, the air seeming to sizzle and burn as it sliced through it, but already Garoch was gone.

"Behind you!" he shouted, reappearing from nowhere. Before the huge blue knight could turn, he thrust the staff into its midst, and the creature screamed and exploded into hundreds of brightly glowing blue shards that flew outwards and melted in the night air.

"Go, go!" shouted Garoch, leaping back into the cart as Pip whipped the horse into motion. Susan helped Tom into the back and leapt in herself as the cart carried over the bridge.

"Two more heading this way!" shouted Pip, glancing about him as he drove the cart further north. Garoch glanced first east and then west, nodding his head as he caught sight of the approaching blue creatures.

"As fast as you can, young Pip!" said Garoch. "I cannot fend two of them off. I was lucky with the one I did."

"Is it dead?" asked Susan.

"Not dead. "Dispersed" is probably a more accurate description. It will regather itself after a time. Not too long a time, I hasten to add."

"Great," muttered Tom, who was once again nursing his arm and grimacing as the cart bumped them around as it fled north,

Pip whipping the horse into a frenzy and Garoch raising his staff and illuminating their way.

"The portal is north and east of here," said Garoch, and Pip turned to look at him.

"How do you know?" he said.

"I can smell it," said the wizard, smiling broadly. Tom wondered for a moment if the wizard seemed to be actually enjoying himself. He certainly seemed to be. "Leave the road between these two clumps of trees ahead."

"Hold on as tight as you can!" shouted Pip, and Tom groaned as the cart bounced wildly across the ground and left the road behind. Susan grabbed at the side of the cart to steady herself.

"There!" she shouted as a bright blue flash illuminated the trees to their left. "It has caught up to us!" Tom looked to his side of the cart, and another flash, but this time, slightly ahead of them, ripped through the trees to the east.

"On the other side too!" he shouted, and Pip suddenly veered the cart left and through a small clearing, Garoch swaying wildly about him on the running board, the staff swinging wildly as the cart bounced across the undergrowth.

"Do you think you could warn me if you are going to do something like that, please?" hissed Garoch angrily, "It is my cart, after all. I wouldn't like to be falling out of it, would I now?"

"Sorry," chuckled Pip, glancing at a break in the trees. Then, noticing a break in the trees, he smiled. "Hard right!" he yelled, and the cart skidded in that direction. The blue light to their left shot ahead but lost them for a second. Garoch looked down his nose at Pip, who was studying the ground ahead of them. The wizard sniffed loudly.

"Perhaps a few more seconds warning would be good," he said haughtily.

"Will do." smiled Pip, and they raced through the trees.

"Ahead now!" shouted Garoch, looking through the darkness ahead. Three groups of trees. Faster, now." He paused, peering across the wooded fields. "There. A single tree."He shook his staff, and ahead of them in the darkness, a small circle appeared in the air, growing larger by the second. It looked like a swirling whirlpool of green light hanging eerily in the dark.

"The portal!" shouted Pip as the two blue shapes reacted to its appearance. They headed directly for the cart, and the increase in their speed was now alarming. Pip stared ahead as Susan and Tom held onto the back of the running board to peer ahead.

"Will we get the cart through that?" asked Tom. "Doesn't look big enough to me."

"Nor me." said Susan, "Much too small."

"It will be fine," said Garoch as the two streaks of blue light solidified in front of them, blocking the portal. They looked like the third had – tall glowing knights of blue lightning, long two-handed swords raised to strike as they approached.

Hold!" shouted Garoch, and he pointed his staff down to the earth. The cart bucked, raised in the air, and shot through the circular portal at great speed.

"Halt!" shouted Garoch as Tom and Susan looked behind them and saw the portal swirling around them. Their surroundings had changed, as had the time of day, for it was no longer night. The field they had been in had vanished. They were on the top of a small hill, a road below them that ran both north and south.

"The portal!" shouted Susan as the whirling circle of light through which they had just travelled continued to swirl behind them. Now, blue bolts of electricity echoed along the whirlpool of light.

"They are coming through the portal!" shouted Tom, "Stop them!"

"Are they now?" said Garoch, and he stamped his staff once on the ground. There was a deep rumble from the ground underfoot, and the circle of light snapped shut and then, in a small burst of light, disappeared altogether. Of the two blue creatures, there was no sign.

"There we are," said Garoch. Told you it would not be hard to escape."

From the back of the cart, Tom could be heard groaning in the bright sunlight.

"Log out, Avalon," he said quietly. Susan sighed as she began to feel the aches and pains she had acquired during their flight across the fields. Tom was still there.

"They cannot follow us as the portal is closed," said Garoch as they gathered in a circle around the small fire that Pip had built to eat some of the food he had hurriedly packed before they had set out.

"What about the road?" asked Tom. "You said you arrived by road."

"Indeed, yes. But that road is for I alone. The likes of them cannot travel that way."

'What exactly are they, then?" said Pip, "You seem sure that they obey the rules of around here, yet I have never seen or even heard of anything like them. Have you?"

"Not precisely," sniffed Garoch, "But we have to make certain assumptions to continue. We cannot continue without food and rest. So, we shall take our chances."

"What do you mean, "Not precisely"?" said Tom. "You either have or you haven't." Garoch rubbed at his beard, clearly struggling with how to explain. After a small pause, he continued.

"Their armour is familiar, as are their weapons. The Urlish knights of the King of Urland wear armour in such a fashion and bear similar weapons. Yet the blue maelstrom that surrounded them? Of that, I have never seen the like in all my days."

"Sounds like you were right about the anti-virus using parts of the simulation to fit in then," said Susan. Tom was rubbing his arm and clenching his fist. "Is that any better?"

"A lot, thanks." he said, "It's still a little stiff, but it is much better than last night. Or yesterday. Or a few minutes ago. Whatever this bloody game considers to be yesterday, anyway. Give it a little time, and it should be back to normal, I reckon." Susan nodded a smile on her face.

"So where is this Ur-land, then?" she asked, and Garoch pointed vaguely north.

"That way." he said, "More or less. Hundreds of miles, though. Why resemblances of Urlish knights are roaming here is a mystery to me. One I am not so keen to pursue, I must say."

They settled into silence as they tucked into one of the sweet-smelling loaves that Garoch seemed to have an abundance of somewhere on his cart that nobody else seemed to be able to spot. Pip had brewed a strong, sweet drink on a pan over the fire, and they drank it thirstily. Susan thought it tasted slightly like tea, but it was very refreshing and left a sweet, rosy taste in the mouth.

"So where exactly are we?" said Susan.

"Puddleswat," said Garoch, a smile crossing his face. "The southernmost county of the province of Southmere. To the North of here is The Mence and The Downs, which leads into the South Wilds and then our destination, Havenholme."

"How far is Havenholme?" asked Tom.

"Oh, I would say perhaps one hundred and twenty miles or so, give or take a mile," he said wistfully.

"A hundred and twenty miles?" shouted Susan, "Are you kidding me?"

"No." said Garoch, "Why would I do that?"

"Oh God." she said, "Just wait until I get to speak to Dylan whatshisname in technical support. He is going to need to lie down for a week at the very least." Tom chuckled.

"I am sure it's not his fault. It's just an adventure, after all."

"An adventure?" she said, her voice rising even more, "One hundred and twenty miles of God knows what, and you call it an adventure? That virus killer stroke glowing blue knight could have killed you earlier. And now we find ourselves stuck in the woods with two rejects from Middle Earth. Forgive me if you think I am being a little harsh, but a nice meal and a good long bath would suit me much better."

'I am just trying to say that we must make the best of what has happened. If we can manage to set a good pace, there is no reason we can't be back to our normal lives in a day or two."

"There is a small sword in the rear of the cart under the blankets. Feel free to arm yourself." Said Garoch, raising an eyebrow towards Tom. "Just a precaution, of course." Tom nodded uneasily. "Try not to lose this one." Smiled the wizard.

"Tell me about Puddleswat," Susan said, facing Pip, apparently eager to change the subject and ignoring Tom and Garoch and any talk of weapons altogether.

"It's no good asking me," said Pip. It's mostly all new to me, too. Everything I know is just a story."

"Well." said Garoch, "As I said, Puddleswat is the southernmost county of Southmere." He stood and pointed his staff north across small drumlins and rolling hills to the road that disappeared into the hills in the distance. "It is a county of little consequence, yet its hills and valleys and green pastures assuredly lend themselves to crops, so the fields are abundant with wildlife. Once we reach the Mence further north, the ground will be much rockier, with cliffs of stone and tall tors of granite. Puddleswat, however, is a place where the land is gentle and good pasture for all beasts of the fields: cattle, sheep, and so on. It is a country largely untroubled, and its dangers are few and slight. There are, of course, those creatures that would prey on cattle, and so we may see Ri-Foxes and the like. Yet they are generally shy of people and stay away. As long as our blue friends keep away, our journey through this part of the world should be swift and true.

"So, no trouble at all?" said Susan, and Garoch gave a brief smile.

"Oh, I think you will find I didn't quite say that," he smiled.

"Hit me with it then," she said. Garoch stared at her, completely puzzled.

"What are the dangers, she means," said Tom.

"Ah. I see. Well, there are only slight dangers, really," said the wizard, "Some of which I have touched upon already. Puddleswat is such a gentle and quiet country that it is very easy to become complacent; lower your guard, and of course, there are always those who would take advantage of such a thing."

"Such as?" said Tom.

"Well. There were rumours I heard not so long ago when I was staying over Havenholme way that a small group of bandits had moved into the hills north of here. They watch the roads for likely pickings, it is said. Of course, it is probably all stuff and nonsense. I have seen nothing of the sort myself, and I have been that way several times. I am sure that we shall be fine."

"I have no idea why that doesn't fill me with confidence, so I shall let it go just this once," said Susan. "I take it that the further north we head, the more dangerous it becomes?"

"Not necessarily." said Garoch, "Though more dangerous than Puddleswat, for sure, yet nothing like as dangerous as any of the counties of Northmere. Havenholme is, of course, as its name suggests, a haven of sorts, and so the lands of the South Wilds are to some degree moderated by its proximity to the city. I would say that the route you take is much more important in those areas. Those who wander off the road are in danger of never being seen again."

"Great." mumbled Susan, "Just great." She stood and checked her dagger was in its hilt. She pulled it from its sheath and tested the sharpness of the blade. Satisfied, she replaced it back in the hilt. She walked across to the cart and climbed onto the back of it, slowly followed by Tom, who gingerly clambered aboard and settled himself next to Susan. Garoch jumped up and took the reins as Pip kicked the last embers of the fire away. Smoke rose from the hill but soon dispersed as he extinguished the fire.

"Ho!" shouted Garoch as Pip clambered up onto the running board. The cart began to move slowly down the hill, swaying as it did so. "North!" he shouted to the horse, who flicked an ear in annoyance. Then they hit the road and swung north, rising through the rolling green hills of Puddleswat.

www.ingramcontent.com/pod-product-compliance
Lightning Source LLC
LaVergne TN
LVHW010120170826
845678LV00012B/2508

* 9 7 9 8 2 3 0 2 3 5 7 3 6 *